RETAKING
ELYSIUM

A Mars Consortium Story

I0626574

M. DARUSHA WEHM

Retaking Elysium
by M. Darusha Wehm

published by *in potentia* press 2020

ISBN 978-0-9951048-6-0

BOOKS BY M. DARUSHA WEHM

NOVELS
Beautiful Red
Children of Arkadia
The Voyage of the White Cloud

Andersson Dexter novels:
Self Made
Act of Will
The Beauty of Our Weapons
Pixels and Flesh

SHORT FICTION
Modern Love and other stories
Retaking Elysium

MAINSTREAM FICTION BY DARUSHA WEHM
The Home for Wayward Parrots

Devi Jones' Locker:
Packet Trade
Sea Change
Storm Cloud
Floating Point

Mars is good place to reinvent yourself, isn't it?

The entire planet is being reinvented every day—domes built, mines excavated, entire branches of science and engineering devoted to remaking the face of the planet in our own image.

It is a world in transition.

Perfect for someone like me.

Chapter One

Earth Aerospace Authority
Interplanetary Transportation Authorization

Knowingly providing false information on this application is an offence under International Law, subject to various penalties.

Destination: Mars colony.
Industry: Mining.
First Name:

The diminutive individual clad all in grey typed into the form, their finger trembling slightly after J-U-L. All their life they'd gone for the letter I next, but then... then it got complicated. Neither A nor O had ever fit right, E wasn't even an option, and X was cool but they knew it wasn't their name.

They took a breath and typed it out for the first time.

J-U-L-E-S.

Last Name:

This was easy, at least. Jules typed quickly then hit the "Next" button.

You have entered **Jules Morales**. Is that correct?
Yes
No, make changes

Make changes. That's what this was all about, wasn't it? Jules was making all the changes they needed to. They hit "Yes."

Preferred pronouns:
They/Them
Zie/Zir
She/Her
He/Him
Other (please specify):

Jules didn't hesitate. They knew this was right for who they were now. They chose the first option.

Documentation complete for applicant **Jules Morales**. Submit their form now?

Yes
No, change names
No, change pronouns

Jules caught their breath. This was about more than changing jobs, more than changing names and pronouns. They'd done most of those things before; it was almost as if change was baked into their DNA. But this was different somehow. It was more.

Who would ever have guessed that filling out forms could be so emotional?

They mashed the "Yes" button, then authorized the form with a thumbprint, wondering not for the first time how secure that really was. It didn't matter. They were Jules Morales and they were on their way to Mars.

⚥

"So, you're off to greener pastures, huh?" Carla stabbed at

the tabletop menu to order another round. The rest of Jules's now-former colleagues had left the party already, but Carla seemed to be in it for the long haul. They were only work-friends—Jules and Carla had never socialized outside of a work event, but they had spent most of their free time at AutoUber together.

"Literally the opposite," Jules laughed. "I'm going to Mars."

If her glass hadn't been long empty, Carla would have spit beer. "You're shitting me."

Jules shook their head as the hatch opened in the wall of the booth they were still hogging, and a jug of beer slid out. Jules poured and said, "I've got a contract in the platinum mines. Room, board, a free rocket trip plus a share of the ore. It's a sweet deal. If I stick it out for a year, I'll be set."

Carla narrowed her eyes as she pulled her now overflowing glass toward her. "*You're* going to be a miner?" She was incredulous, and waved her hands wildly to indicate Jules's body. "Give me a break. You're like... tiny." She said it as if they might somehow have gotten this far in life without noticing their relative size.

Jules took a long pull on their own beer before answering. "Do you actually think folks are taking pickaxes to the rocks up there? This isn't the Dark Ages. I'm mainly going to be controlling robots. It's not that different from what we did at AU. If I have to actually do anything physical, I get to wear an exo."

"Come on," Carla said. "I watch *Bodyshop*. I've seen those Martian slabs of beef. Some of these people with their muscular augments..." She let out a breath and fanned herself with her free hand. "They'd pick you up and sit you on their shoulders like a parrot."

It was a surreal image and Jules couldn't help but laugh. "Sure, there's some call for muscle jobs. But I'll be in a different area. I mean, obviously." They imitated Carla's hand-waving.

"Okay, I believe you," she said. "I couldn't do it though. Leaving everything, leaving the planet! It's too much, even for all the gold on Mars."

"It's platinum."

"Whatever." Carla took another swig, then leaned in. "So, Space Cowboy, you wanna come back to my place and knock one out?" She grinned and arched an eyebrow.

A couple of years of mild office flirtation lessened Jules's surprise at the offer, but Carla was loaded. So was Jules for that matter, and they shook their head. "We better not." They lifted their glass and pointed at it.

"You're probably right," Carla said, raking her eyes over Jules's exposed arms. "It's just that I always wanted to see the rest of the tattoos."

♂

Another jug of beer later Jules gave Carla her wish in the autocar, after covering the hidden cameras their insider knowledge revealed. Jules lay back on the bench seat in their underwear, the pinging of the car's seatbelt alarm piercing their ears until they realized they could just buckle the clips underneath.

Carla's proposition was long forgotten as she took in the art on Jules's body as if it were a canvas—or an entire gallery.

Her hand hovered over a particularly well-realized

watercolour cube. "Can I touch?"

Jules nodded. "It doesn't feel like anything," they said. "Just skin." Carla's finger lightly traced the ink lines, and Jules shivered. All thoughts of sex were gone, now. This was something different.

"You can take a holo," Jules said impulsively. They'd never done anything like that before; never done anything like this at all. Sure, plenty of people had seen them naked, but not like this. Not so deliberately. Was it the knowledge that they were leaving which made them comfortable with so much vulnerability, was it some desire to, at last, be truly seen? Was it just the epic quantities of beer? It didn't matter. It felt right.

Carla beamed and grabbed her handheld. "Turn your head," she said. "And cover your face." It was no guarantee, but it might help keep the image from being automatically connected to Jules's online profile. "I'll know it's you," she added as she snapped a few shots.

They hugged when the car stopped outside Carla's building, then Jules was alone. The short ride back to their apartment was eerily quiet without Carla there, and a drunken lucidity came over them. Everything they did for the next three days would likely be the last time they'd do that on Earth. Every step would be numbered, the countdown ticking ever closer to zero. Jules never stayed anywhere very long and figured that they would return to Earth one day, but right then, as the car swished to a stop outside their building, it felt like an ending.

An ending, but as they always are, it was also a beginning.

New name, new planet, new person.

Chapter Two

"Call me Lisa Marie," she said to the shift supervisor. It wasn't the name on her credentials, but she hadn't gone by that in years. She liked to mix it up and no one had ever cared if the moniker you used matched your forms. Over the years she'd been a Tabitha, a Cinnamon, a Gale, a McNulty, a SparkleStar, and a Dayne. She'd forgotten half the names she'd answered to, and that was how she liked it. New place, new name. Nostalgia was an addiction and she did everything she could to keep artifacts from the past from intruding into the present.

"Sure," her new boss said, making notes on her handheld then leaning back in her chair. The first time Lisa Marie had tried that on Mars she'd nearly flipped herself over backwards, the lighter gravity making her misjudge her own strength. Her boss, Sanders, had it down pat, though; booted feet landing squarely on the corner of the small pull-down desk in the site office. It was hardly an office at all, roughly carved from the rock in the underground mine where they worked. Lisa Marie guessed that it hadn't been done specifically—the niche felt more like the result of the early mining efforts before PlatinuMars™ had built the infrastructure that made mining a more efficient and frankly much less demanding pursuit.

Sticking an office in a literal hole in the wall was exactly the kind of thing that they would do.

"You'll get your schedule for the next ten sols on your personal feed," Sanders said, "and after you've been with us for a couple of rotations you can see Housing about your apartment upgrade."

"I know the routine," Lisa Marie said and Sanders nodded.

"Let me know if you need anything," Sanders said and let the handheld fall to the desktop. She stood and stuck out a hand for quick shake. "Welcome to the team."

♂

The path back to the train station was well-marked and mostly even underfoot. Lisa Marie remembered when it wasn't quite so safe—she'd been among the first crews when Mars was opened up to non-specialists. There were essentially two kinds of people on those first shuttles: adventurers who'd have done any kind of job if it meant they could go live on another planet, and people who were desperate. She was among the latter, much larger, group.

Lisa Marie had always worked so-called "unskilled" labour, the same as her parents before her and their parents before them. Like most people she worked with she'd never had enough free time and available credit for further formal education and without those credentials she was never going to get past the front door for a tech job. That had never bothered her much in and of itself—she didn't mind the work so much as the lack of opportunities.

She had done a lot of different things in her life for a paycheque, and was willing to work in strange circumstances. She'd had more than a few jobs that paid very well for what they were, but the problem was always what to do when they ended. She once went over a year without anything more than a few nights' side hustle running deliveries. Even big money from a stint on a remote project didn't last that long when you have to pay rent, buy food and keep your body running. Her whole adult life she'd had to have one eye on the next thing, but even then it didn't always work out. When her last Earth-bound construction job had ended, things had looked bleak. Her savings were down to the last few Euros when she heard about PlantiuMars™.

When she arrived, there were only two habitation domes and a single administration dome. The Entertainment Zone opened shortly after her group had arrived and there were only a few amenities in those first months. As she walked along the well-lit path with its high-vis safety markings and instructional panels written in several languages, she marvelled at how far along they'd come in less than a year. Even in the mines it was often easy to forget you were on another planet. Only the emergency environmental suits and warnings about what to do if there was a perimeter breach brought the reality home.

The small train station was uncrowded since it wasn't a shift change time. She'd only been by to check in with Sanders before her first shift the next day. It never hurt to be a little eager when you started in a new team. The flashing lights went off and the *ding-dong* sounded just before a train pulled in, and she stepped aboard. The car was still new and shiny, no signs of the debris and vandalism you saw on public transport on Earth. She slipped into a seat for the short ride to her dome.

The Mars Consortium—the groups of companies which

owned PlantiuMars™ and which ran the infrastructure on the planet—had done a good job of simulating Earth daylight in the domes, but it wasn't exactly right. It reminded her of those enormous indoor malls on Earth that mimicked a last-century outdoor environment, with cool breezes and green trees. They both had that little hint of the uncanny valley. But as employer-provided housing went, the domes on Mars were more than decent.

She walked from the station to the open centre of the dome, where there was a small green space struggling to take hold, benches and tables scattered around, and a few carts selling food and trinkets for company scrip or platinum shards. She picked up a salad of hydroponic microgreens and a freshly baked croissant, and found a table.

As she forked a clump of sprouts into her mouth she sensed a presence behind her. As she turned, a soft voice said, "Heard you're moving on up in the world."

She looked up into the craggy face of a guy she'd worked with on the rock line, her old job. He was older, and seemed a little odd; he kept to himself mostly. That was common—you probably didn't end up sorting rocks on Mars if you were an outgoing people-person. If she'd ever known his name she didn't remember it now. There hadn't been a lot of socializing on that team.

It was boring but easy work—making sure that the raw ore on the sorting line ended up in the big hoppers. Computers did the work of determining the quality of each chunk of ore, but the movement of rocks along the conveyor belt was erratic enough that some pieces managed to make their way out of their slots, so human intervention was still required. She figured there probably was a more efficient automated solution, but everyone had to start somewhere. It was probably cheaper for the Consortium to hire low-skilled labour for a long-term commitment to Mars, with a training and promotion program, than it would have been to develop an automated system and only bring skilled workers on board. Besides, why they did things they way they did was well above her pay grade, even at her new job.

"Yeah," she said, gesturing for him to join her at the picnic table. "Level up." She made the *bing-bong-boop* sound from an RPG that had become popular in the new gaming arcade.

He nodded. "I'm holding out for a triple," he said, referring to the practice of taking an exam which allowed a person to skip two levels and go straight to a senior position. "Passed the test, just waiting for a vacancy."

Lisa Marie nodded, not particularly interested in this guy's career strategy, but it was best to be polite. It was a small community and you never knew who'd end up being next to you in an emergency situation. Or who might become your boss. *Bing-bong-boop*.

"Don't know how long you've been here," he want on unbidden, "but it's just starting to come together. The new hab domes are going up now, the scientists all moving into Admin Dome 3 to get started on the terraforming project. I heard they're opening two new bars and a dance club in the E-zone." He shook his head as if he couldn't quite believe it. "Gotta say, I kind of feel like the other shoe's about to drop."

"What do you mean?" Lisa Marie knew she was opening herself up to a potentially endless conversation—this guy was obviously in the mood to talk—but she couldn't help herself. She was curious.

He shrugged. "You hear things. Like the Consortium might be taking bids on an outside license."

"A license for what?"

"Who knows? Commercial stuff for the workers, habitats for rich Earthers? Could be anything." He looked off into the distance, through the clear dome window over the tunnel tube to the adjacent dome over the dun-coloured rock outside. "Anything but mining rights, probably. Can't see the MC giving them up."

"Huh," she grunted, "sounds like idle speculation."

"Ha!" he barked a laugh. "Speculation! That's a good one."

"Oh," she said after a moment's pause. "A mining joke."

He ignored her comment and stood up, pushing himself away from the table. "We'll just have to see, eh? Catch you around." He wandered off and she went back to her lunch. He'd disappeared into one of the habitation towers when she realized she still didn't know his name.

Oh well. Names didn't mean much, after all. As she pulled her croissant apart, she stared out at the view he'd been so interested in—brown rocks, a hazy sky. She thought she could make out Elysium Mons in the distance, but it could have been her imagination. There honestly wasn't much to see. It was hard to believe that for most of human life this view was literally the stuff of dreams, while to her it was just another ordinary day.

Chapter Three

Jules closed their eyes against the scenery rushing past the window. The hyperloop to the Quito space elevator ran above ground most of the way as it gained altitude, and while Jules was sure the view was interesting, the speed made looking out the window impossible. If they were nauseated on the train, how were they ever going to manage spaceflight?

They turned away from the window and flipped open their handheld to stare at the Earth Aerospace Authority clearance again. All stamped and duly noted: one passage to Quito orbital and one berth on Mars Consortium shuttle *Burroughs,* baggage allotment 21.64 kg.

The extra four and a half kilos were payback for all those years Jules had strained to see in a crowd and failed to find clothes that fit in the adults' section. At first it hadn't seemed hard to get everything they wanted to take in the single soft-sided duffel they were allowed to bring. Mars had access to all the holo stations for both Earth and Luna Colony, so they didn't need books or movies. They would be given a uniform for work and the living quarters were supplied with cookware and basic furniture. But cramming an entire life into 17 kilograms was an incredible challenge, and in the end Jules used every gram of their extra ration. For spaceflight, at least, it paid to be small.

The train began to slow enough for Jules to comfortably look out the window, but the view had become dominated by the anchors and struts for the elevator. Jules couldn't see the thick cable running high into the heavens, or the car which transported people and goods up to the orbital. But there were no end of solid metal beams and the large electric trucks painted in garish high-vis colours and festooned with blinking lights. It was heavy industry as far as the eye could see.

"I'd better get used to that," Jules thought. Mars wasn't likely to be much different.

♂

One day the elevator station would probably resemble an airport in a hub city, but now the service kiosks and niches where cafés and shops would be were empty or being used for storage. Flimsy printed signs were tacked up to indicate the path through to the cars, but the flow of people from the train made the direction obvious. Luna was slowly starting to become a tourist destination, but the planned resort hotel on the orbital had developed a funding crisis the previous year and that stopped work on most of the visitors' infrastructure here.

As Jules looked around at their fellow travellers, they figured that almost all of them were going to space for work. They joined the queue for the next car and scanned their EAA authority at a terminal near the entrance to the waiting room. Their bag was passed through an inspection machine and their biometrics were read half a dozen times, but it was efficient enough that they still had to stand around to wait for a car to return from the orbital.

It was so thoroughly mundane that it was easy to forget what was happening. They were about to board a vehicle which would shoot them into space, where they'd get on an honest-to-goodness spaceship and go to Mars.

When they were a kid, this was the stuff of adventure holos. And now it was a lucrative, if somewhat unusual, means to hopefully ridding themselves of years of debt and maybe even getting ahead.

What a time to be alive!

⚥

The trip up to the orbital reminded Jules of the beginning of those carnival rides that drop you into freefall, when the car shoots up to the top of the apparatus. Of course, it lasted a lot longer, and Jules hoped that there was no freefall part. When the car stopped, after the light over the doors turned green and the safety belts disengaged, Jules stood and carefully took a step. They thought they felt lighter, but it was hard to tell. They joined the throng of people entering the orbital and looked around for the way to their shuttle.

If Quito station felt unfinished, the orbital seemed more like it was never meant to be anything more than a working dock. Jules understood why the resort's backers pulled out— there weren't even any windows. What was the point of being in space if you couldn't see the stars?

They found a tattered, crooked sign with the Mars Consortium logo on it and an arrow pointing down a dimly lit corridor. Jules shouldered their 21.64 kilograms and set off in search of the *Burroughs*.

They had to stick to the walls, as there were cargo handlers moving crates on forklifts driving down the middle of the hall, and they were beginning to wonder if the sign had been pointing in the wrong direction when they saw an open hangar door. They peered inside to find a dozen people seated on folding chairs, their own baggage at their feet. A uniformed functionary with a ruggedized handheld looked up.

"EAA authorization?"

Jules pulled up the form and the official scanned the document. "Morales," she confirmed and Jules nodded. "Grab a seat if you can find one. We're waiting for a few more people, then we still need clearance to launch. It'll be a while."

"Okay." Jules turned to where the other people were waiting, but the chairs were all occupied. It wouldn't hurt to stand for a while, they figured. After all, they were about to sleep for months. Plenty of time to rest on the way.

♂

It was just over an hour later when Jules found their seat on the shuttle. It was odd, sort of like a recliner, with a glove-like feature on the left armrest. They got settled and a different uniformed attendant helped them strap in. "You'll be awake for a few hours at take off and landing, but the captain will tell you when to get ready for the sleep."

"Uh," Jules looked up at the guy in his Mars Consortium jumpsuit. "How does that work, exactly?"

A smile creased the fellow's face, creating a pair of rather fetching dimples above his thick and glossy beard. It was quite disarming, and Jules appreciated that they picked someone for this job who was so distracting.

"Your hand goes in here," he said, lightly guiding Jules's hand toward the glove, without actually sliding their fingers inside. "There's a monitor and, I'm not going to lie, a needle. You'll feel it, but it's not bad. The drugs will knock you out and there's an IV for nutrition and hydration while we're underway."

Jules nodded. This whole process had seemed a lot less terrifying when it had been theoretical, but the attendant had obviously seen plenty of people with the jitters before. He gave their hand a squeeze and the smile lit up his face again.

"This isn't first class travel, but it's better than banging around in zero G for months. I've done it dozens of times. You'll be fine, promise."

Jules almost believed it.

The purpose of the orbital was so that there was no gravity well to escape, so takeoff was anticlimactic. The dull metal of the orbital simply appeared to fall away, and the vast sphere of the Earth became visible. There were gasps from all around Jules, the image of Earth from space still utterly awesome to many who saw it. Jules found themselves unable to turn away from the window until the Earth had receded to a tiny speck and the view was, as they say, full of stars. They were still staring out the window when the PA crackled to life and a kindly voice said, "Welcome to space, folks. I'm your captain for this quick four month flight to Mars. I'll be setting the autopilot in a few minutes, then it's going to be lights out for us all for a while. If you could all get comfy with your hands in the envelopes, that would be great. Trust me, you don't want to be the only one awake for this trip—we've all but run out of coffee and pretzels."

The person next to Jules nervously laughed, then slid their hand into the glove.

Jules did the same, then said, "See you on the other side."

"I sure hope so," the other person said, then Jules felt a sharp pain in their arm. The whole ship seemed to spin ever so slightly and Jules only had the time to think that they'd never even introduced themselves to the person they were going to be sleeping next to for the next few months.

Chapter Four

"What do you mean, you *hope* something will come up soon?" Lisa Marie's nostrils flared and she took a deep breath. She knew that the poor sap on the other side of the counter didn't have any control over the housing assignments, and getting angry wouldn't help. But she *was* angry.

"I mean there isn't a single available Level Two apartment on Mars," the guy said, looking genuinely apologetic. "Hab dome four was meant to be completed by now, but..." He shrugged. "There are a few people ahead of you on the wait list already. I'm sorry. This affects all of us."

Lisa Marie drew a breath to argue, then closed her mouth. It was not this guy's fault. For all she knew, he was missing out on his own upgrade.

He seemed to appreciate her restraint, and said, "I know this sucks; you're entitled to a Level Two and it's part of your contract. But there just isn't one. I've heard that the Consortium is thinking about some kind of compensation, but you'll have to talk to someone in Pay and Banking about that. All we can see here is the housing stuff."

Lisa Marie sighed. Bureaucracies were the same everywhere, no matter what planet you were on. The Housing Directorate guy tapped at his screen and her handheld vibrated in her pocket.

"I've set up a notification for you so that you'll know where you are on the wait list," he said. "It won't get you an apartment any quicker, but at least you won't have to come back here and wait in line."

"Okay, thanks," she managed to get out, even though she didn't feel grateful. Everyone on Mars was making a lot of money, being paid in shares of the platinum being mined and sold by PlatinuMars™. But on an everyday basis, money didn't mean much on Mars. She and everyone else received scrip for food, clothes, and anything else that was for sale through the Consortium. You could pay platinum in the underground economy, which was growing but still tiny, and a person would have to go through an awful lot of sketchy homebrew drugs to make a dent in even a Level One salary. Besides being bored with your job, apartment upgrades were the biggest incentive to move up in the organization.

She left the Housing Directorate office, and walked through the Administration dome in a daze. She had to dodge queues of people on her way to the station—there didn't appear to be a single office that was able to handle the number of people who needed their help.

It's just growing pains, the rational part of her mind told her, as she squeezed between two different lines of people trying to get into the Uniform Allocation Office. When she'd first arrived on Mars, the single Admin dome had seemed incredibly ambitious: ten levels of offices, with front counter staff and administrators, even security personnel. It felt like there had been three bureaucrats for every other person on the planet.

But now it felt as if overnight the population on Mars had exploded. It wasn't overnight, of course. But two brand new mining sites had opened since Lisa Marie arrived, and it seemed like there were shuttles transporting new people to the planet every other sol. Mars was booming, and it was going to take some time for the infrastructure to catch up.

As she waited on the crowded platform for the next train, Lisa Marie knew this was normal. She knew it was virtually impossible to plan an expansion perfectly. There would always have to be some areas ahead or behind others. It would pass. And compared to the scrape and struggle just to find a decent job on Earth, this was a life of luxury.

But why did it have to be *her* apartment upgrade that was delayed?

She couldn't face going back to her tiny Level One apartment with its narrow cot and fold-down table. In her darker moments, she thought the only thing that made it an improvement over a prison cell was the door to the combination shower/toilet cubicle—and the fact that she never had to be there. So, she used that freedom to ride out to the large dome where the shared recreation facilities were all housed. People had started calling it the Entertainment Zone, now that there was quite a bit more than a gym and a cafeteria.

As she walked through the dome, past the cafés, bars, a proper sit-down restaurant, the holo theatre and games arcade, Lisa Marie had to admit that maybe the Consortium had gotten this part right. She reluctantly acknowledged that if she had to choose between a nice apartment and a good selection of things to do elsewhere, she'd have picked the E-zone, too.

She'd worked in a closed environment before, helping to

build a solar farm in the wilderness of northern Canada. Facilities for the staff to use in their off hours had been an afterthought at best, and even though their housing and pay had been good, almost everyone got cabin fever. There were only so many nights she could spend on her recliner, watching the wide screen holo. For most people the main source of recreation had been flirting, sex and relationship drama, but she wasn't interested in any of those activities. For her, it was cannabis and holos and that was about it.

As she found her mind drifting back to those years, she forced herself to pay attention to her current surroundings. If she weren't careful, she'd find herself zoned out, lost in the details of some dumb comedy or a banal conversation with a solar electrician she'd never see again.

A fake-wood sign reading "Coming Soon" caught her eye and she wandered over to the construction. There was no door on the space yet, so she peered inside, to see the beginning of what looked like it would be a high-end whisky bar. The memory of a smoky, golden flavour washed over her and she caught herself.

Single malts had been her thing when she called herself Dayne. She was Lisa Marie now, and she wasn't about to let herself get caught up in memories she couldn't possibly recreate even if she wanted to. It was another time, on another world. She was here to move forward, not get caught in the amber of memory.

She tuned away and focussed again at the options open to her here and now. What did she want? Why was she here?

A throb of bright lights caught her attention and she began walking toward it, but it felt like too much. Loud music and the crush of bodies didn't appeal. She walked past the dance club toward a nondescript door and a flicker of light. It looked like an old-fashioned neon sign, but as she got closer she saw that it was a holo. It read, simply, BAR.

She pushed open the door to find a classic dive, with a few low tables scattered around the room and stools at the long bar. Another fake neon holo above the bar spelled out REST in green letters, and over the door where an EXIT sign would be was the glowing word WORK.

"What can I get you?" the woman behind the counter asked as Lisa Marie walked up to the bar. "We've only got these going right now," she added, gesturing to about half of the gleaming taps, "but there are plenty of bottles if none these grab you."

She'd never been much of a beer snob before, but it was never too late to try something new. "I'll have a pint of the IPA," Lisa Marie said, and the bartender nodded.

"Hope you like hops," she said, as she pulled the pint.

"Me, too," Lisa Marie said, and she turned to the room. It wasn't crowded, but it wasn't quiet either. She noticed an area in the back with another holo blinking out PLAY over a couple of pool tables. It certainly wasn't glamorous, but it seemed like a decent enough place to hang out. Maybe she'd even take up playing pool.

Chapter Five

The recruiters never said space travel would be glamorous, but they never said anything about the vomiting, either. Jules wiped their mouth with the back of their hand and carefully stood. As they'd disembarked at the shuttle airlock, an attendant had handed them a small pack of some kind of gel, the instructions on the wrapper indicating they should swallow it in a single shot. Jules hadn't had a chance to even tear it open before their stomach lurched and they had to follow the bright orange line to the nearest toilet facility.

Now they leaned against the cubicle wall and, in that brief respite that came after losing the contents of their stomach, they fumbled with the pack and managed to slurp down the goo. At first, they thought it wasn't going to take—the sensation of the viscous mass sliding down their throat was utterly vile—but whatever pharmaceutical sorcery was contained in the stuff worked its magic and Jules could literally feel their stomach unclenching.

They rinsed out their mouth and left the cubicle, running right into the cute attendant from the shuttle.

"Sorry," they said, bouncing slightly off the man's solid chest. They managed to notice his name tag now, which read *Hassan*.

"Don't sweat it," he said, grinning. "Between the reduced gravity and everything else," he waved his hands over his stomach in a fluttery motion, "it's easy to get discombobulated when you first arrive."

"Yeah," Jules said, glancing back at the row of toilet cubicles, "that was a bit rougher than I expected."

Hassan nodded. "It gets better with practice," he said, "but not much. At least I usually manage to get the 'Welcome to Mars special' down the hatch before I have to take a trip to Chunder City." He held up a crumpled package matching Jules's own empty gel shot container. "Better living through chemistry, right?"

"Right." Jules looked up at him, knowing full well that the stirrings of feelings were really just a reaction to this man being the only person on the planet with whom Jules had exchanged more than a few words. That, and Hassan's remarkable attractiveness. At that moment, Jules could have spent a lifetime looking into these deep, brown eyes. But they knew it was fleeting. Of course, everything was fleeting.

"Look," Hassan said, as if reading Jules's thoughts, "I'm only on planet for a couple of nights before it's back to the grind, but why don't I show you around? It will take a while for you to get settled, and there's more here than meets the eye." He pulled out his handheld and tapped at the screen. "You have proximity turned on?"

Jules fumbled for their own device and poked at the settings. "Yeah," they said, and a contact notification with what looked like a link to a map popped up.

"If you're up for it, meet me here tonight," Hassan said and turned away. "It'll be more fun than space sickness, I promise."

"Okay," Jules said as Hassan walked away. His long legs and the light gravity combined with an innate grace made it almost look like he was dancing. Jules had no doubt that by that evening, they'd be up for it, whatever it was.

Jules found their way to the intake office and joined the line up of new recruits. Everyone looked a little green around the gills, and someone near the front of the queue had to make a run for the toilets. The recruitment holos never showed anything like this. But Jules was feeling better every moment, and the queue was moving steadily. Soon Jules was at the counter, facing a friendly—if slightly bored looking—Mars Consortium Staff Officer.

"Intake form?" The woman behind the counter gestured for Jules to pass over their handheld. She scanned a code, then tapped at her workstation. "Jules Morales, mining drone programmer, Level One?"

"That's me."

She nodded and tapped some more. "The lock code for your apartment has been sent to your handheld, plus there's some maps of the domes and an explanation of the transit system. You'll have an orientation tomorrow, but don't worry, it's nothing too taxing, and it won't take the whole sol." She gave them a grin. "We know it takes a while to get used to everything."

"Okay." Jules frowned. "Uh, the whole soul? What's that?"

She laughed. "A sol is a Martian day. A bit more than 24 and half Earth hours. We still divide it by 24, so a Martian hour is a little longer than an Earth hour. So, if it feels like time is dragging on, that's because it is."

"I guess that explains the high hourly wage, then," Jules said and she laughed.

"It all works out—the workday is longer, but the breaks are, too." She handed Jules back their handheld and said, "There's a direct link to your Consortium account on there now. If you have any questions, that's the first place to look. Welcome to Mars."

$$\sigma$$

Jules found their apartment easily thanks to the map, but they probably wouldn't have had any trouble without it. There were only three open habitation domes, named simply B1, B2 and B3, and they were right next to each other. Their apartment was in B1 and there were signs everywhere. The interior of the dome had apartment blocks circling its edge with straight vertical faces toward the centre of the dome. As Jules looked up, they could see the curvature of the dome along the open edges between buildings, making it clear that the higher floors offered less space. That explained their apartment number: 923.

They walked through the central open area toward the door marked B1-5, noticing a handful of people making use of the benches and tables near the spindly trees. It was not entirely dissimilar from Jules's old neighbourhood, but there was no mistaking it for Earth. The air smelled wrong. Not bad, exactly, but strange. As if the seaside and an airport had a scent-baby.

Jules chuckled at the notion as they swiped their handheld over the reader at the door to the building. It clicked open and they walked through to a small vestibule with two corridors leading off toward the ground level apartments, and an open spiralling lift system. They hopped on to the next step that flipped out of the central tube, and rode up.

They passed several identical floors before stepping off on level nine. It might be small, but it was technically a penthouse. They found 923 and tapped out the numeric code from the orientation document. *CHANGE THIS PASSCODE* flashed from the device as the door unlocked.

Jules stepped inside and immediately froze. Partly because the entire apartment could be traversed in only a couple of steps, but mostly because of the view. The entire exterior wall was a window, looking out over the Martian plain. Ochre rock filled their view, with the peak of one of the mountains visible in the distance. Jules really ought to learn the names of some of these features, but it could wait. They stood and gaped at the alien view for a long time.

Eventually, they snapped out of it and took the grand tour. One interior wall had a small table attached to it with hinges, with two built-in chairs that flipped out from the tabletop. Next to the table was a tiny fridge, reheater and set of cabinets. On the opposite wall there was a tack-board where the previous occupant had left a pin-up holo. Jules appraised the image of the naked but modestly-posed model. Whoever used to live here had good taste, at least.

Jules pressed at the top of the tack-board and the whole unit popped out of the wall with a hydraulic hiss, then folded down to reveal the narrow bed. It barely cleared the table and with them both down, and the room was nearly completely filled. Okay, so it wasn't the Ritz. But the view was priceless.

⚥

After a quick shower in the tiny bathroom, Jules went in search of the bar where they were meeting Hassan. At least, they assumed it was a bar. That seemed like the kind of thing that a mining colony might have. When they got off the train at a station with a new-looking sign marked "Entertainment Zone," they wondered how much entertainment a place like this could really offer. Maybe *two* bars?

There were more than two bars.

Hassan's directions led them to a place with a thumping bass line, a dim interior aside from the strobing lights, and a glittering sign out front that read "Sequins." Did Hassan want to meet at a dance club? They walked in and couldn't help but croak out a laugh. It *was* a dance club, but it was the kind where you sit and others dance.

Up on the central stage were three people in various states of undress, doing frankly amazing things on a pole, a trapeze, and aerial silks. Jules found Hassan at a table near the bar and slid into the seat next to him.

"Incredible what you can do in lower gravity, isn't it?" Hassan said, eyes on the stage.

Jules debated what they wanted out of this evening, what they wanted from Hassan. They weren't entirely sure, but they didn't want to rule anything out just yet.

"I don't know," they said, leaning in toward Hassan, close enough to smell the oil he used on his beard. "But I wouldn't mind learning."

Chapter Six

It smelled like spilled beer, roasted soybeans, and algae. The last was ubiquitous, of course, as the recycled air in all the domes had that briny tang. The rest was classic bar smell, and Lisa Marie was beginning to find it soothing. It smelled like relaxation, like conversation, like companionship.

She took her beer to the back of the bar where she joined a knot of off-duty miners. She recognized all of them, though only knew a few by name. One of whom was now the centre of attention—a petite, rosy-cheeked transport driver called Cap. They were dressed in their usual off-duty riot of colour: a pair of jewel-toned paisley-patterned jeans with an emerald green button-up under a gold bomber jacket. It should have been migraine-inducing, but they wore it well.

"Lisa Marie," they beamed as they caught her eye. "I'm glad you made it."

"Wouldn't miss it for the world," she said. "It's not every day that one of our own hits the big time."

Cap laughed. "You have seen the shuttle I bought, right? It's more like Tiny Time." She had seen a holo of Cap's new ship. Well, it was new to them, anyway. It had more dimples than an orange and, now that it was Cap's, she guessed that it wouldn't be long before it was the same colour. But to be able to buy one's own shuttle, even second-hand, was something she'd never thought she or anyone in her position would be able to do. There was something to be said for working on the edge of human habitation—it paid really, really well.

"So, when are you blasting off on your intergalactic tour?" a voice from the crowd asked.

"I'm leaving in two sols," Cap said, "though it's not exactly going to be a leisure cruise. I've already got a cargo run to Luna booked in, then I need to pick up some other work in a hurry. I spent every shard I had on that shuttle, so I have to start the hustle. But now that Mars is going to have a tourist trade, there should be plenty of opportunities for an independent operator."

Ripples of conversation spread around the crowd. "What are you talking about?" Lisa Marie asked.

"You haven't heard?" She shook her head. "The Consortium sold a licence to build a resort south of the new hab domes."

"Not just a resort," someone else chimed in, excitement in their voice. "A hotel and casino!"

Someone snorted. "There's talk of a golf course. It's ridiculous."

"How can they be building all that when they can't even manage to get us our housing upgrades?" Lisa Marie asked.

"It's not the Consortium building it," Cap said. "It's a private Earth company. The Consortium just sold a licence."

"But what about the infrastructure? Breathable air, filtered water? Surely it won't be completely self-contained."

Murmurs went around the group, and no one seemed to know the answer. Lisa Marie was pretty sure she knew. There was no reason why the Consortium would need to licence a completely stand-alone project on Mars. If this company wanted to build a resort, with their own landing facilities and environmental systems, they could just pick another patch of planet and do it. They had to be relying on Consortium infrastructure.

It was a sell-out, that's what it was.

The conversation turned, and she finished her beer. Lisa Marie was no longer in the mood for a party, so she wished Cap well and left the bar. Going back to her tiny Level One apartment was only going to make her more angry, so she needed to do something else.

Most people took the train loop between the domes, but there were pedestrian tunnels connecting them all as well, so she put one foot in front of the other and walked.

The come-ons from the many venues in the E-zone were having the opposite of the desired effect on her, and everywhere she turned she found herself annoyed. So Lisa Marie walked away from the bright lights and into the tunnel connecting this large dome with the adjacent administrative dome. The walkway was nearly a kilometre long, the domes spaced out widely to accommodate construction and repair facilities around them. There were armourglass windows at intervals along the edges, and an eerie blue light shone through. Sunset.

She stopped to look at the pale white dot at the base of a sky which reminded her of a stormy day on Earth, the blue-grey colour making the alien planet at once familiar and foreign. Sunrise and sunset always felt strange on Mars, stranger than day or night. It was, she reflected, a reminder of what she missed of Earth.

She'd loved to stare up at a clear blue sky whenever the

opportunity presented itself, the openness of it contrasting with the bustling world of the cities below. Other than her stint in the Arctic, she'd always lived in a city, with their relentless motion of people and things. Cities were like living systems, that required constant maintenance and change in order to stay functional. They were never truly silent. But looking up at the sky, Lisa Marie could imagine a place where nothing beeped, no one shouted, and the movement of the few clouds were dictated by cycles of weather, not the demands of survival.

She didn't know how long she'd been standing at the window when she forced herself to stop. If she let herself go, she'd get lost in the memories, caught in a spiral of daydreaming about the past so much that she'd lose track of her present. It didn't matter that the memories were mundane. It happened even when she found herself remembering moments that were boring, or unpleasant. It's not that she thought the past was better or more interesting —it was that once the memory took hold of her, she found it so hard to refocus on anything else.

She shook herself, fully, like a dog shaking off water. She didn't care if anyone saw, but there was no one else in the corridor. She needed to feel her body now, with all the aspects that made her Lisa Marie acting on it: her sore right shoulder, the Martian gravity, the slight artificial breeze from the air recycler. She made her hands into fists and took stock of the way her muscles felt. This is who I am, she told herself.

She walked with purpose toward the next dome, concentrating on the details of the tunnel. Here, where the joints in the fabricated walls were sealed; there, where the wheels of a drone cart had scuffed the floor. By the time she got to the tunnel's exit, her thoughts of Earth had faded. She knew that they were still there, like a dormant virus waiting for a dip in her immune system. But for now, she was here. On Mars, walking through the nearly deserted domes alone.

Chapter Seven

After their first night on Mars, Jules didn't expect to see Hassan again. He'd left on the next shuttle run and Jules figured that would be it. But instead their friendship continued the next time Hassan was in port, though they didn't sleep together again. Hassan wasn't interested in romance—his life was complicated enough without a partner.

"I'm on the move too much," he'd said. "I feel like I have one foot on each planet, and I like it like that. Besides, I spend most of my life zonked out on a shuttle. It's months between when I take off and land. I don't want to change my life for someone else and it's not fair to ask someone to put up with me only part time. It's better for everyone this way."

Jules agreed. They hadn't been looking for a boyfriend; it had just been one of those one-time things. Jules was no stranger to one-time things. And between the novelty of being somewhere so completely different, and the heady intoxication of a friendly and beautiful face in a literally alien environment, Jules taking Hassan back to their tiny bed was no surprise. But since then, the two of them often got together when Hassan on planet. It turned out that they actually liked each other, even without the novelty and the pheromones working their magic.

In those first few months on Mars, Jules found the days— make that the *sols*—seemed to fly by. In fact, when Hassan messaged Jules to say that he was back on the planet, Jules hadn't believed it. How could eight months have gone by already? But between learning the ropes at a new job, finding their way around the colony, and meeting new people, the time just disappeared.

"I don't think I've even seen a single shard of platinum," Jules said, gesturing with their chopsticks as Hassan dove into his own bowl of noodles. "My work is so far removed from the actual mine, it's almost like playing a holosim."

"There are real people down there, though," Hassan said between bites, and Jules nodded.

"Sure, the drones and robots can only do so much. But they do a lot, especially the more dangerous and physically demanding work. I can't imagine that this could be profitable without them." Jules picked at the floating bits of protein supplement floating in their soup. They didn't know exactly what it was, but it tasted good. "I don't know if it would even be possible. There's only so much a human body can do."

Hassan nodded. "It's appropriate somehow that robots still live here. After all, for the longest time they were the only things that lived here."

Jules laughed. "I don't think I ever would have put it that way," they said, "but you're not wrong."

They finished dinner, then Hassan said, "So, what's new since I was here last? It's almost like every time I have shore leave on Mars there's a new dome up and running."

Jules thought. "There is a new hab dome, finally. But that's not very interesting, unless you're one of the people who was on the wait list for a new apartment. Then it's the most interesting thing going."

"Surely something fun is going on," Hassan said, eyes

twinkling. "Besides housing upgrades."

"I did see something new in the E-zone," Jules said. "Come on, let's check it out."

They took a few wrong turns in the large, bustling dome before Jules recognized it. The door was nearly hidden between the flashing lights of a holo-sports arcade and a dance bar, but the glitter of some material designed to look like cut glass finally caught their eye. Etched into the "glass" was the name "Robinson's" spelled out in cursive script. They pulled on the bronze door handle, and the fake wood door opened to a small, dark bar.

It was reminiscent of something Jules had seen in an old video, with wood panelling, small tables, candlelight and velvet. Music played just loudly enough that you couldn't easily overhear the people at the next table, but not loudly enough to really make out the song. About half of the tables had couples or small groups at them, engaged in low conversation. They found a table for two near the bar and the tabletop menu system illuminated discreetly when they sat.

"I... don't know what I'm looking at." Jules said after studying the scrolling list. "I don't even know how to pronounce half of these things."

"It's a whiskey bar," Hassan said. "I mean, that's what most of what's on the menu, anyway." He swiped his hand over the tabletop. "There's other stuff, too." He tapped to flip the menu to show Jules what he was looking at. "Cocktails, some wines and beers. Fancy sodas."

Jules recognized a few items. "Do you think they bring this stuff all the way from Earth?"

"Some of it," Hassan said, then squinted at the fine print. "Looks like a lot is synthesized here, though. You want to try something?"

Jules nodded and let Hassan order for them both. When the drinks arrived, Jules eyed the small measure of amber liquid barely swirling at the bottom of the glass. "Add just a touch of water," Hassan said and demonstrated with his own drink. "Then take a little sip."

It reminded Jules of dirt. Not in a particularly bad way, but it was nothing like the sweet maltiness of the beer they would have chosen. On the second sip, they caught more—a light sweetness, the astringent alcohol taste. "Not bad," they finally pronounced. "But I think it's an acquired taste, and I'd rather spend my extra scrip on something I already like."

"Fair enough," Hassan said, then something caught his attention in the distance, and he stood. Jules turned to see a tall, fit, and quite attractive white man approach the table, a wide smile on his face. He looked vaguely familiar as he embraced Hassan and accepted a lingering kiss on the cheek.

"Marvin," Hassan said, "this is my friend, Jules. You want to join us? Uh—" Hassan shot Jules an apologetic look, as if realizing that he hadn't checked to see if that was okay. Jules grinned back and nodded, then reached over to the next table for another chair.

Marvin sat and said, raising an artfully groomed eyebrow, "Don't let me interrupt anything."

"You aren't," Jules said. "Hassan was teaching me about whiskey, but I'm really more of a beer person."

"Well, you should come over to the dive bar where I work," Marvin said. "We have a dozen beers on tap, not to mention pool tables and the occasional free amateur boxing match."

It took Jules a moment to realize that he meant a bar fight. They laughed when they got it, and Marvin grinned.

"What's it called?" Jules asked, pulling out their handheld for the map.

"The sign at the door just says BAR, so we've been calling it The Mars Bar." He paused for a beat. "It's pretty sweet."

"You are terrible," Hassan said. "If the dancing doesn't pan out you should go into comedy."

That was when Jules figured out where they'd seen Marvin before. He was one of the strippers at Sequins.

Well, knowing Hassan, that fit.

A few weeks later Jules was on the lift after shift with a couple of other people from the autonomous team.

"You checked out the casino yet?" the tall, darker-skinned one asked.

"Nah," the other one said. "Doesn't really seem like it's meant for us, you know?"

"Screw that. No one is going to kick us out." They turned to Jules. "Have you been?"

"No," Jules said. "Not really my thing."

The other person snorted. "That's what they want you think, but our money spends as well as those space tourists' does. Come on. Let's go!"

Jules shot a look at the third person in the lift who made a "What can you do?" face. "I've got plans, sorry," Jules said as they reached the main floor and scurried away before they could get roped into a work outing. "Let me know how it goes."

They got a train to the E-zone, even though they didn't, technically, have plans. It was more of a notion, but they definitely preferred it to going all the way out to the Elysium with a pair of random coworkers. They followed their handheld's map until they saw it: the fake neon BAR sign. They pushed open the door and walked into the dim room.

It took a moment for their eyes to adjust, but then they saw him behind the bar, turning on the charm for a group of people who looked like they were also just off their work shift. Jules hung back until the crowd had passed, then walked up to the bar.

It took him a moment to place their face, but then the 1000 watt smile returned. "Jules!" Marvin said, reaching over to almost but not quite touch their arm. "You made it!"

"It seemed to me like this was the place that had what I wanted," they said.

Chapter Eight

It wasn't everything that Lisa Marie had wanted, but when she unlocked the door to her new apartment it was as if the gravity had reduced another third. Just that slight bit of extra space between the bed and the table, and the addition of an armchair by the window made her feel like this was double the size of her old place. There was room to breathe, now. It wasn't luxury, but it was liveable.

She dropped the duffel bag that contained all her personal possessions on the floor and took it in. The closet with an actual door. An area that you could probably call a kitchen if you were feeling generous. Space for two people to sit comfortably. With the bed folded up, you could get another couple of chairs in there. Hell, she could throw a party if she wanted to.

She put her things away, made a cup of tea, and sank into the armchair. She stared out the window, the umber landscape stretching out before her. She could just make out the shuttle docking station in the far distance as another spacecraft arrived. She couldn't see it well enough to watch it maneuver on to the docking arms, or see the airlock bridge extend out to allow passage from the shuttle to the docking facility. She certainly couldn't read the markings on the hull. Regardless, she was pretty sure it was another commercial liner carrying tourists for the new resort.

The *Elysium*. How dare they?

It probably wouldn't have mattered what they'd called their stupid resort, she would have hated it. But it pissed her off that they had co-opted the name of the place where she lived. Where they *all* lived.

The entire human habitation of Mars was contained within a relatively small area of Elysium Planitia, in the shadow of Elysium Mons. "Elysium" belonged to everyone, not just the few people who could afford a trip to Mars and a few nights in a five-star hotel room.

She sipped her tea and popped the recline function on her chair. She'd just moved into her new place, she was supposed to be enjoying her newfound comfort, not getting riled up about this casino. She had a long shift the next day breaking ground on a new vein of ore, and she needed to rest.

She started a meditation program on her handheld and followed the voice prompts, paying attention her body and her breath. It was so easy to get caught up in her own head, to lose herself to memories or anger or worries about what might happen. She had to fight every day to stay connected to the present. At least she finally had a comfortable chair to do it in.

$\male$

"Watch out!"

The chunk of Martian rock flew past Lisa Marie's face, centimetres away from her nose, and smashed into the digger robot working next to her. It shuddered to a stop, internal machinery calibrated to shut down automatically when it was damaged. In what felt like slow motion, she turned toward it to see the indentation in the bot's chassis, a shallow crater the diameter of a dinner plate. She remembered to breathe as the sound of shouting voices came to her as if from the bottom of a well.

"Are you okay?" Her workmate, Nicos, shouted into her face as he grabbed her by the shoulders. She took stock of her body.

"Yes," she said, once she thought it was true. "It missed me."

Nicos let out a breath, still gripping her shoulders. "That was close. Look at that dent. That could have been your head."

"What happened?" she said, still staring at the broken bot.

"That's what I want to know." The shift supervisor, Sanders, strode over to Lisa Marie, her heavy brows meeting in the middle of her forehead. "The debris alarm was going off for half a minute before that boulder went flying. What were you doing here? You need a hearing check?" That last question could have been said with a nasty irony, but it was clear from Sanders's tone that she meant it. The heat had gone from her voice and her role as the caretaker of her staff had clearly reasserted itself.

Lisa Marie shook her head. "My hearing seems fine. But, I didn't notice it so... maybe?"

Sanders sucked her teeth and dug out her handheld. She poked at it harder than was necessary, maybe taking out some of her frustration on the defenceless device.

"I'm booking you in for medical. Just in case, okay? That was too close and it shouldn't have happened. I need you 100% on this line or not at all, understood?" Lisa Marie nodded, still not entirely sure what had just happened. "Go home. Medical's first thing tomorrow, then we'll see."

"Okay." She grabbed her stuff and turned toward the

roughly hewn tunnel from the new dig site back to the main mine and the train station.

"You need a hand?" Nicos asked, falling into step beside her.

"No thanks," she said, "I'll be fine. Don't lose your shift on my account, really." He looked at her, clearly debating with himself if he believed her, then finally nodded once and turned back to the site.

She made it home with no further incidents, except a knot of anger at herself growing ever larger.

There was nothing wrong with her hearing. She'd been fairly certain at the time, and the medical the next day confirmed it.

"You sleeping okay?" the medic asked after the battery of tests were complete. "Fatigue is one of the main causes of distraction."

"I've been sleeping great," Lisa Marie said and it was true. Her new apartment was an upgrade in every way, including comfort. It didn't have anything to do with fatigue. She knew what it was. It was a relapse.

She fought down the shame that crept up as the realization took hold, and said, "I was caught up in a memory. It's a problem I have sometimes; I kind of lose myself. Can you give me a recommendation for a counsellor or something? Do you have those here?"

"Of course," the medic said. "But there's nothing wrong with daydreaming, exactly."

"I wasn't daydreaming! This is different," Lisa Marie said, her discomfort morphing into anger at having to fight for the help that was so hard to even ask for. "It's a known issue. I've had therapy before and it helped. Can you just give me a referral, please?"

"Sure," the medic said after a pause, and in a moment her handheld buzzed with an appointment. "I'm sorry about questioning you. I'm more of a scrapes and bruises doctor."

Lisa Marie nodded, the rush of adrenaline ebbing from her bloodstream. She was probably going to need a nap. Sleep really wasn't her problem.

♂

Her shift supervisor let her back on the line and, if anything, Lisa Marie was over vigilant in the days between the accident and her appointment with the therapist. There was only one counsellor for the entire planet, and she had to wait her turn. Until she could get in, she had to just focus, force herself to stay rooted in the present.

When she was on site, she jumped at every little noise, double and triple checking her work. By the end of her shifts, she was so tired that all she could manage was to get back to her apartment and crash. But that was better than falling down the rabbit hole of her memories, and it was a lot better than nearly being brained by a chunk of Mars.

Chapter Nine

"Hiya!" Marvin called as Jules walked into the Mars Bar at the end of their shift. "I'll be done in a few minutes. Can I get you a beer before I'm off?"

"Sure," Jules said. "I'll grab a table." It had become a regular routine on the days when their work shifts coincided, which between Marvin's two Consortium jobs and his side hustle, wasn't all that regular. It didn't take long for him to finish the shift change and pull a couple of pints before Marvin slipped into a chair next to Jules.

"Happy Tuesday," he said as they clicked glasses.

"I think it's Thursday," Jules said and Marvin shrugged.

"It doesn't really matter what you call it. I just do what my schedule tells me to."

"I'll drink to that," Jules said, and did. They'd had multiple jobs before and knew how complicated it could get. They hated having to switch from one mode of thinking to another, and had been happy to get a full-time gig at AutoUber that paid enough to get by without needing side work. The complexity of his work life didn't seem to bother Marvin, though.

"I haven't met many other people on Mars with two jobs. Is it just more common in hospitality?"

Marvin shook his head. "I could get more hours here or at Sequins if I wanted. But I'd get bored if all I did was pour drinks, and I don't know how long my joints would hold out if I danced much more than I do. And on top of that, I like working for myself. Keeps me out of trouble." He winked and Jules felt heat creep into their cheeks.

It's not as is they didn't know what Marvin's third job was, and it's also not as if they thought there was anything wrong with it. But Marvin being a sex worker made Jules think of sex. And Marvin. And what sex with Marvin might be like... and there was the hot-in-the-face feeling. They took a long sip of cold beer.

"So, how does that work?" Jules asked, eventually.

Marvin's eyebrows rose. "I'd hate to disabuse you of any notion you might have that Hassan is in any way discreet, but I'm afraid he told me a few stories which make me think you have a pretty good idea how that works."

Jules laughed and the awkwardness faded slightly. "I mean the money part. Here, we can spend Consortium scrip, same as at Sequins. But your other work isn't through the Mars Consortium, right? So, how do you get paid?"

"Ah. Well, the short answer is platinum. There are a few folks selling goods or services on their own now. More every day. Since you can't transfer scrip to another individual, we give each other platinum." He leaned back in his chair. "After all, that's how the Consortium is paying us."

Jules frowned. "Sure, but I've never seen any actual platinum. It's just a number in an account somewhere that goes up every payday. It could be platinum or Euros or New Dollars. What it's called doesn't really matter."

"Oh, but it isn't the same at all," Marvin said, enthusiasm creeping into his voice. "There are all these interesting fiduciary rules about currencies, which is why you can't transfer scrip. The Consortium isn't allowed to have its own currency, so that figure in your account represents literal grams of actual platinum metal that you could go and get from the Pay Office. They are required to give you shards or bricks if you ask for them. Some people even do! I have a few clients who pay me in bare metal," Marvin grinned. "I don't know if it's for anonymity or just the fun of it, but I've got nearly a kilogram of platinum in my apartment. I really should bank it, but I never seem to get around to it."

"I had no idea," Jules said. "About how any of this works, or that you were so into economics."

Marvin laughed. "I'm a giant nerd," he said.

"It's cool." Jules took a pull on their beer. "You, know, it's weird. So much of the time life on Mars doesn't really seem all that different from the way things were on Earth, but then —blammo—something totally strange comes up like this." They shook their head. "I wonder what else I don't know."

"If you have any other questions, I'm happy to share my wisdom." Marvin beamed that grin again. Jules took another sip of beer, the coldness of the liquid and the effects of the alcohol steeling their nerve.

"Yeah, I do actually. What do you charge?"

Marvin's face twitched and Jules thought they saw the genial mask of the consummate service worker slip for a moment. It wasn't unpleasant at all. "That depends on whether you're asking out of capitalist curiosity or personal negotiation." He didn't let Jules answer before continuing. "If it's curiosity, my base rate is 10 grams of platinum an hour. There's a bit of flexibility for good customers, unusual requests, that sort of thing. But if it's a personal inquiry..."

Marvin paused and Jules had the impression that he might be nervous. They'd never seen Marvin look nervous. It was disconcerting.

"If it's personal, I should tell you that there are some people I won't accept as clients. Because I'd rather have them as..." Marvin looked like he was searching for the right word, then failing. "Non-clients?" Jules wasn't sure what he meant until they felt Marvin's hand lightly rest on their knee.

"If I've gotten the wrong impression, please tell me," Marvin said.

"No," Jules answered, the breath catching in their chest. "You've got it right."

"Oh, good," Marvin said and let out a breath. "I know it might seem strange, but is it okay if we take things slowly?" His hand hadn't moved from its perch on Jules's knee, but the ease and warmth of his light touch felt nice.

"It's very okay," Jules said, sliding their hand on top of Marvin's.

They got another round, Jules telling horror stories about programming autocars, Marvin holding forth on a variety of esoteric subjects.

"So, what's the big deal about this casino?" Jules asked. "Everyone's talking about it as if aliens landed or something."

Marvin let out a sigh. "If only," he said, his voice losing its characteristic lightness. "As employers go, the Consortium isn't that bad. We're all making a lot of money here, and it's not a bad place to live. But it's like an old-fashioned company town. It's not like I can just take those kilos of platinum I have and say, 'Here's some cash. Give me a Level Four apartment.' I'm stuck with the quarters I've been assigned and there's no amount of money that can change that. Which is okay—this is complex system and what passes for free market economics work here even less well than they do on Earth. But then they go and give a licence to Jacoby Enterprises to build that monstrosity of a resort. It's..." He struggled for the right word. "Disrespectful. And it's bad business."

"Why? They paid for the licence, right? So that's just more money for the Consortium."

"Sure," Marvin said, "but up here most problems are the kind money can't solve. There's only so much infrastructure here, and we're already increasing capacity as quickly as we can. Unlike on Earth, if we're overcapacity, we can't just move. Without the domes, and their life support systems, we'll die. So all of us up here making Mars profitable and, more importantly, *livable* are stuck with this," he waved his arms around, "while the tourists who come up here get to have their luxury resort and casino experience. All the money they spend will get siphoned back to Earth into a Jacoby Enterprises tax-sheltered investment account. Meanwhile we're stuck with waiting lists for housing upgrades." He polished off the last of his beer. "It's kind of bullshit."

"I don't really get it," Jules admitted, "but you aren't the only one who seems pissed off about it."

"I'm not," Marvin said, and took a breath as if to say more, then seemed to think better of it. "But you don't need to listen to me rant about economic injustice all night. What do you say I walk you home?"

"Okay." Jules stood and Marvin took their hand, his

fingers squeezing lightly before relaxing. Jules twined their fingers with his, and they walked out of the Mars Bar hand in hand toward the train station. It reminded Jules of being a teenager, the thrill of being seen publicly with someone hot who clearly liked them.

When they got to the door of Jules's apartment, they stopped. "I'd invite you in," Jules said, "but my place is so small that there's no pretence of going slow when there's nothing but a bed in there."

Marvin grinned. "That's okay, it's getting late. Thanks for a nice night." He paused, looking Jules in the eyes. The light in the hall seemed to dim, as Marvin moved ever so slightly toward Jules. They could feel his breath, and moved toward him millimetre by millimetre, the moment stretching on as if it might break. Then, finally, their lips touched and Marvin kissed Jules with a light, chaste touch which left Jules nearly painfully wanting more.

But Marvin turned, slightly flushed, saying, "I better go. I'll talk to you tomorrow?"

"You better," Jules said, their voice husky, as they tapped out the door code quickly and fled through the open door into their apartment before they could turn back to Marvin and forcefully drag him inside.

Chapter Ten

Lisa Marie looked through the open door and wondered if the therapist, Dr. Singh, needed help more than her patients. Her dark hair had nearly fully escaped from the braid which had once constrained it, and her golden earrings were not exactly a matching pair. On another person it would simply be their style, but Lisa Marie didn't think the doctor had intended the look. Regardless, she was smiling and professional as she ushered Lisa Marie into her office.

"I'm sorry to keep you waiting," she said, downing a cup of coffee and tapping furiously on her handheld. "I'm busier than a one-toothed man at a corn-eating contest."

The folksy non-sequitur made Lisa Marie laugh and Singh smiled as she sank into her chair. "Glad to see your appreciation for bad jokes is intact," Singh said, waving her into the chair opposite her desk, and scanning her handheld. "Says here you like to be called Lisa Marie, she/her pronouns?" She nodded. "So then, Lisa Marie, what's up?"

She'd have preferred to warm up to the topic a little, but her appointment was for only twenty minutes, and she figured there won't be an opportunity to extend the time. She took a breath, closed her eyes, and forced it out. "I get obsessed with my memories. I've always been this way, but I thought I had it under control. I'd been doing better—I was able to stop the loops from taking over. But it's come back now, all of a sudden, and my usual techniques aren't working."

"Are these particular memories?" Singh asked. "Specific incidents you're reliving?"

Lisa Marie shook her head. "They're just random thoughts from my past; nothing terribly interesting or traumatic or anything, just events. It's always been like this: moments from my life come back, like I'm watching a movie, and I can't seem to look away."

Singh nodded, but didn't say anything.

"It's always a problem when this happens, you know, for my general mental health. But now it happened on the job and it nearly got me injured. I'm worried that it's getting worse."

"You've had therapy before," Singh asked, "for this issue?"

Lisa Marie nodded. "I've never had a formal diagnosis, but one of my counsellors called it Nostalgia Loop Disorder."

Singh nodded again. "It's not a recognized condition yet, but I've read a few papers about it. For some people it's characterized by always referencing the past, as if it were more real than the present or future. For others, it's an overwhelming sense that the best is behind you."

"That's not me," Lisa Marie said. "I'm not all about the good old days. I just... when a memory comes, I can't stop thinking about it. Or, I *can*, but it's difficult. I have to really work at it. And lately it's getting harder."

Singh nodded and made some notes. "Let's look at this from another angle. Tell me about some of your plans for the future," Singh said. "After you're done working for PlatinuMars™, what's next? Working the mines isn't an easy way to make a living. What are you saving up for?"

Lisa Marie frowned. "Nothing in particular? I like

physical work and I liked the idea of being somewhere remote, somewhere new. Besides, when this opportunity came up I was flat broke. It was Mars or bust, for me." She paused, but Singh didn't fill the silence. Finally, Lisa Marie said, "This wasn't part of a grand plan, it was just a job. That's how things have always gone for me—I've never really had enough security to plan for anything."

"Not even a pie-in-the-sky, what if I found a bag of money on the street dream?"

Lisa Marie thought about it, then shook her head.

"I see. It's hard enough staying in the present, right?"

"Yeah."

"Well, the present is kind of a slippery thing," Singh said, leaning back in her chair and popping her feet up on the corner of her desk. "Some people believe it doesn't even really exist, from either a physics or a philosophical standpoint. But the future *is* real, at least in our minds. In the sense that when we imagine what might be, and strive to work toward that goal, we are creating a situation where that outcome might become possible. We shape ourselves and our surroundings in a way that makes that imagined reality more likely."

"Like greasing a track," Lisa Marie said.

"Exactly. Trying to stay rooted in the present is hard—there's a reason why being in the moment is a meditation exercise. But if you find something you want to achieve, something you want to change, and work toward that, it might help ground you in the day-to-day. And if you have more to focus on now, that may help make it easier to resist the desire to return to past memories."

A bell dinged, and a slight frown crossed Singh's face. "I'm sorry, that's our time. I'll schedule you in for a follow-up, but it's going to be a while from now, I'm afraid. You'd really think that they'd have expected a little more work for therapists up here. I mean, it's not exactly a surprise that there's more than a few cases of Earthsickness, but..." She threw up her hands in an exaggerated shrug. "What do I know? I'm a doctor, not an administrator."

Lisa Marie bumped the door to the bar open with her hip, squinting at the dimness inside. She'd hoped that Dr. Singh would have given her some kind of exercises to do, Cognitive Behavioural Therapy or something. A specific action she could take when the thoughts got out of control. But, of course, she already had those tools and they hadn't been working for her. There was no simple solution, no injection to counteract her stupid brain. We could send people Mars but we still couldn't stop brains from being jerks.

Her eyes adjusted to the dim lighting and she made her way to the bar. She recognized the bartender on shift, the same woman who'd served her that first pint of IPA when the place had opened. Lisa Marie had been coming regularly enough that she knew the woman was called Ylla, and that she did, in fact, like hops.

"We've got a new XPA on. Give it a try?" Ylla asked, a frosty glass already in her hand. Lisa Marie nodded and thanked her, then leaned against the bar as Ylla poured the drink. "Tough day?" Ylla asked as she carefully set the brimming glass down on the mat.

"Not really," Lisa Marie said. "No more than usual,

anyway." She took a sip of the beer and smiled in appreciation. "Nice."

Ylla nodded. It was in between shift changes, so there was no one else waiting at the bar. "The hydro farm is finally getting some new crops out. The Riwaka hops grew like gangbusters, so the brewers really went to town on this one. It's a bit too green for me, but the hopheads seem to like it."

"Yeah, it's good," Lisa Marie said. "Citrusy."

"Well, enjoy it while it lasts," Ylla said. "Word from HQ is no more experimentation in the farms for the next season." She rolled her eyes. "Gotta focus on 'core production' only." She made air quotes with her fingers.

"Well, we do have to eat," Lisa Marie said, but Ylla snorted.

"You see anyone starving? Food production is fine. They just don't want to expand, give us anything a bit more interesting than the basics. It wouldn't be hard to pop up another greenhouse dome, let the biotechs try something new. But instead they're building that new admin dome so a bunch of bureaucrats can work out how to sell licences to Earth corporations to build a fucking theme park."

"Someone's building a theme park on Mars?"

Ylla barked a short laugh. "No, it was just an example. Though, honestly I wouldn't be surprised if someone did in a few years. That resort is planning a golf course, so who knows?"

"Wow," Lisa Marie said. "That is a bit ridiculous."

Ylla nodded. "Someone ought to do something about it. I mean, without all of us who live up here, PlatinuMars™ can't make any money. The Mars Consortium is supposed to be looking out for us, making things liveable up here, but it seems like they're more interested in selling chunks of the planet off to the highest bidder. It's like they forgot they actually need us."

"Yeah," Lisa Marie said, the germ of an idea forming in her mind. "Someone really should do something about that."

Chapter Eleven

"Ugh," Jules said, the twinkling of the alarm ringing forcing them out of the depth of sleep. "Can you do something about that?"

It felt like a tiny marsquake hit the bed as Marvin rolled out of the other side to find the source of the noise. He eventually found Jules's handheld under the table, and tapped it silent. Jules opened an eye to watch Marvin pad around the apartment, his one-piece sleep suit hugging his body here and there. It was much more effective than the alarm.

"I don't want to go to work," Jules complained as they shuffled up to a sitting position, but Marvin had disappeared into the bathroom. Jules stretched and accepted the reality of the morning, and set about finding their clothes. By the time Marvin returned, Jules was dressed and tugging on one boot.

"Thanks for letting me stay," they said, suddenly shy. Marvin bent down, took Jules's chin in his hand and lightly kissed their lips.

"Thank you for not pushing," he said, softly, tracing a finger over the neckline of his outfit.

"Of course," Jules said, then ran their eyes up and down Marvin's body. "Besides, I've seen you naked before. Along with half of Mars."

Marvin smiled and stepped back. "You've seen me without clothes," he corrected. Jules didn't entirely understand the distinction, but they knew it meant something important to

Marvin.

"Keeping it casual is fine with me," Jules went on. "We'll have fun while it's fun, and that's it. Nothing lasts forever, right?"

Jules thought they saw a change in Marvin's eyes, but his smile never faltered.

"I'd better get going," Jules said. They had to get back to their own apartment, shower and change before making their shift at work. It would be tight, but it had been worth it. "I'll stop by the bar after work?"

Marvin nodded. "I'd like that," he said, then kissed Jules again, longer this time. It was hard to leave, but Jules managed. Eventually.

It was a tough shift, between the new quotas they were asked to meet and Jules's lack of sleep. But they made it through and found themselves perking up at the thought of seeing Marvin again.

The Mars Bar was already starting to get crowded when Jules arrived, and they knew that Marvin still had a few hours on his shift. They didn't want to make more work for him by getting in the way, so after saying hello and getting a beer, they scanned the room to see if there was anyone else they knew.

A bunch of the miniature giants Jules's old coworker Carla had gone on about were hanging around the pool tables in the back. Jules wasn't sure there was any actual billiard game in progress, and the voices were developing the volume that indicated that either a fight or a declaration of love was about to break out. Maybe both. Jules found a corner to lean against out of splatter range to watch the show.

The taller of the two most vocal putative pool players gave the other one a shove, sloshing the only slightly smaller one's drink almost out of the glass. The others gathered around all froze, and Jules found they were leaning forward even though they could see just fine. After what seemed like an overly dramatic pause, the victim of the not quite spilled drink bellowed a laugh and threw an arm around the taller one. Hugs and laughter surged through the group and Jules turned away, pleased that it was all in fun, but secretly a bit disappointed that the entertainment was over. It wasn't that they'd wanted to see an all-out bar brawl, exactly. More that they were getting a bit tired of everyone being so well-behaved on Mars. Where was the passion?

As they sipped their beer, they scanned the rest of the after-shift crowd. The usual knots of workmates winding down were broken up by twos and small groups clearly looking for love or lust. Fair enough—that's why Jules was there after all. As they were pulling out their handheld for a book to pass the time, one larger group caught their eye.

A pale-haired white woman was holding court over a large table filled with people who didn't really fit the other profiles. They didn't seem to be similar enough to be workmates and there was a complete lack of a sexy vibe. She was gesturing constantly but in a reserved manner, as if she were trying to avoid being conspicuous. The others were listening closely, an older compact man occasionally interjecting. For all the world it looked almost like a business meeting.

A hand landed on Jules's shoulder, making them jump.

"I'm sorry," Marvin said, his smile making those adorable

creases at the corners of his eyes. "I didn't mean to startle you."

"It's fine," Jules said, leaning up for a kiss. "You always surprise me."

Marvin frowned. "I do?"

"Mmm-hmm. Keeps things interesting."

"Oh." A slight hint of colour appeared in Marvin's cheeks.

"See," Jules said, triumphant. "That's what I mean. Who would have thought anything I said could make you blush?"

"You know most of what I do is acting, right?" Marvin said, sliding on to the seat next to Jules. "At all my jobs. I'm playing the part of a person who is happy to serve. I mean, even my name is part of the act."

"It is?"

"Sure. Back on Earth, when I was already contracted to come up here but before I left, I was working at this club. My friend Sandy suggested I ought to use it—the whole Mars schtick. So I worked up this routine, Marvin the Martian, complete with green body paint and those deely bopper antennae." He wiggled his fingers over his head and laughed. "It was silly, but folks loved it. Tips were excellent that week."

"How come you still use the name ?" Jules asked.

Marvin shrugged. "I got used to it, plus I've never liked my wallet name. Actually, it was my favourite part of that gig. It was the only part of it which felt like me."

"You do like your work, don't you?" Jules asked, concerned.

"Oh, sure," Marvin said, the confident manner returning. "But it's not the real me, you know? Honestly, that's part of the appeal of all my jobs. I get to make people happy without having to really open myself up. It's a lot less vulnerable than..." He looked away. "Than real life."

Jules took Marvin's hand and squeezed lightly. "Thanks for letting me be part of your real life," they said, softly.

They sat in silence for moment, hand in hand, then Marvin said, "I'm a bit done with the bar scene today. Is it okay if we head out for some food and just have a quiet night?"

Jules grinned, downed the last sips of beer in their glass, then said, "I thought you'd never ask."

They walked toward the door, passing by the table Jules had been watching before Marvin arrived. As they approached, the conversation abruptly stopped, and the woman who'd been talking looked up at them. She and Marvin shared a glance, but didn't say anything to each other. The conversation at the table didn't start again until they were out of earshot.

"You know her?" Jules asked, then immediately back-pedalled. "Sorry, I shouldn't ask that. Your clients are my none of my business—and I'm sure it's not exactly great advertising to see you with me, either."

"My personal life is none of my *clients'* business. I'm not trying to keep you hidden from anyone." As if to prove the point, Marvin pulled Jules in close for a lingering kiss. After breaking free, he pushed open the door to the bar and they strolled through the E-zone, looking for a quiet restaurant.

"But that woman isn't a client," Marvin continued. "She's... I'm not really sure how to explain it. Organizing something, I guess. She approached me to see if I'd be interested in helping out, that's why she was giving me the eye."

"What kind of thing?" Jules asked.

"I don't think they really know yet. Maybe a union? Something to try and get a voice back for the people of Mars."

"The people of Mars?" Jules laughed. "That sounds like some kind of Communist Revolution talk."

"Kind of," Marvin said. "We are in a strange place where there are these really clear divisions up here: there's PlatinuMars™ which owns everything, the Mars Consortium which runs it all, and us. The people who make it all go. We're the only ones without a say in what happens, but without us there is no Mars. At least, no Mars like this." Marvin gestured to the bustling dome full of people.

"So, are you going to help them out?"

Marvin shrugged. "I don't know yet. But I haven't said no."

Jules thought for a moment. "I get the feeling that saying no isn't really a problem for you."

"It's not," Marvin agreed. "I'm pretty happy I didn't say no to you, though."

Chapter Twelve

"No." He wasn't nasty about it, but he was insistent. Lisa Marie gave him the "go on" gesture and the older guy nodded. "We have to stop meeting in public, and the bar is a public place. Even if every single person in this joint is in with us, it's still run by the Consortium. It's not safe here."

"But you just said all that, out loud, here in a Consortium bar," the young East Asian woman next to him said in an accusing tone.

"If they've been listening all along, it's already too late. We'd have been rumbled a long time ago," Lisa Marie said. "I think Smith is trying to make sure we minimize the likelihood of that happening in the future."

"That, and getting away from their ears in case we're wrong and they *are* on to us," the grizzled fellow added.

"Okay," Lisa Marie said. "So, how do we share the new meeting location? I don't trust the messaging on the Consortium net."

"Surely everyone still has external messengers," the skeptical woman next to Smith said.

"Of course, but the Consortium net is always going to be the first node transmitting the message. If we're being paranoid, we need to be properly paranoid." Smith leaned back, a slightly smug expression on his face.

There was no chance whatsoever that Bob Smith was the name on his credentials, but Lisa Marie of all people couldn't care about that. After the first few meetings they'd had at The Mars Bar, she'd recognized him as her old rock line coworker; the one who'd initially told her about the rumour of the Consortium selling an outside licence. He'd been bang on there, and she figured he was still pretty clued in to the current situation on Mars. He'd turned up at the very first meeting she organized, and he'd quickly become her partner in crime.

Well, it wasn't technically *crime*, as far as anyone could tell. The Consortium wasn't a government, so they couldn't be committing treason. It wasn't a military structure, so it wasn't insubordination, and it wasn't a sea or space fleet, so they weren't mutineers. The young woman was an administrator, and she said she was sure there wasn't anything in the standard contract which forbid organizing a grievance committee, advocating for other employees or even unionizing. But they all knew that what they were doing was likely to get them in trouble if it were public knowledge, which was why they were moving their planning meetings to a more secure location.

"We'll just have to do it the old-fashioned way," Smith said. "I'll tell two friends, and they'll tell two friends. But quietly."

Lisa Marie nodded and the administrator grinned. She'd never shared a name with the group, not even pseuds like the others. Smith obviously wasn't the only one with paranoid tendencies.

"Okay," Lisa Marie said. "Catch you all next time, in our new home."

♂

Their new home was an underground room made of natural

Martian rock that had once been part of the original mine. It was large enough for a boardroom table and a bunch of chairs, and was accessible by walking though the labyrinth of the old mining tunnels. And, as of two days from now, it would also be accessible from the storage room of a new café that had just opened.

The newest habitation domes had been built over the old mine, and the café, Normal Bean, was run by one of Smith's pals. Their storage room was right over the dugout, and they'd fitted a trapdoor and ladder as a secondary access. It was the perfect secret location for a quiet meeting of like-minded individuals.

Lisa Marie looked around at the empty room, wondering what would come of all this. It was one thing to get together with a bunch of people in a bar after work, drinking beer and talking shit. It was some next level business to be planning a clandestine meeting in a literal underground hideout. But she had to give all this cloak and dagger routine its due—she was focussed. She hardly ever thought about the past at all, and when memories did come to her, it was easy to push those thoughts away. She didn't think she was cured, but she was doing better again.

That twenty minutes of therapy had really helped. She was lucky, though, that she'd had so much success with only the one session. What about everyone else who hadn't been so fortunate? How many people were struggling with being so far away from their families, or from being able to see a tree that was taller than they were? How many people had ordinary issues that didn't even have to do with being on an alien world, but weren't able to get more than twenty minutes of help in a month—or longer?

This was why they were meeting. It wasn't just having to wait for a larger apartment, or more variety in the noodle carts. It wasn't just that the people who worked on Mars deserved to have their contracts met—they deserved more. And there were real world consequences to not having those obligations met. And it didn't matter on which world they happened to be.

Thankfully, the near infinite exponential progression of information sharing implied by Smith's plan hadn't occurred, but the space was nearly full. Lisa Marie recognized the core group of three as well as Ylla from the bar, but there were half a dozen faces she'd never seen before sitting around the table. The door to the old mine opened and Marvin, the other bartender, walked in with his partner. Lisa Marie arched an eyebrow, but the intention had been to bring in new people. If they had to abandon this meeting space, so be it, but there was no point in driving away anyone who was interested.

"Hi, everyone," she said, once five minutes had passed beyond the scheduled start time. "I'm guessing you all know that the reason we're meeting is because things have gone wrong on Mars. No one expected it to be easy working here, and I'm not going to deny that we're all being compensated rather well for the work we're doing. But money isn't everything."

There were a few murmurs of assent around the table, but also a couple of blank stares. Smith broke in. "Do I think we deserve more than the bare minimum the Consortium is

obligated to provide? Yeah, I do. I admit that. But let's be real
—they aren't even providing that. Sure, there's a decent pizza
joint and live holos, but what about the waitlist for housing
upgrades? What about your clothing allowance: has anyone
here gotten new threads on time?"

"And stars help you if you need non-urgent medical care,"
one of the new people Lisa Marie didn't know said. "I'm a
doctor and we just don't have the people. Even when we pull
longer shifts, there's more demand than supply. That's not
right. Medical care isn't like platinum."

"But, isn't this just growing pains?" Marvin's partner, the
small person with all the tattoos and piercings, piped up from
near the door. "I mean, I doubt the Consortium wants things
to be a shambles—but there's only so much they can do with
what we have."

A few people nodded, and all eyes turned back to Lisa
Marie. "Personally, I don't believe they want this, either," she
said. "But ultimately, the problem is there's no such thing as
the Mars Consortium."

A few people obviously scoffed, and an older black
woman laughed. "Tell that to the folks building the new
admin dome."

"Oh, the Consortium is real, but it's not a single
responsible entity," Lisa Marie went on. "I mean, look. The
Consortium is a big organization with a lot of moving parts.
There are representatives of the corporations who make up
the Board at the top, then a whole group of high level
executives. Then there's everyone else, all the way down to
the people in this room. I'm certain that no one at the
Housing Directorate wants a waitlist. The folks working

dome construction aren't skiving off or delaying on purpose. I don't even believe that those executives back on Earth are trying to deliberately screw us over. But it doesn't matter whether it's deliberate or not—they *are* screwing us over. They are more concerned with maximizing yield, making extra money off corporate licences, than they are with fulfilling their contracts. And that's what I think we should be fighting for."

She looked around the room, and saw a lot of nodding heads.

"In the end, it doesn't matter *why* things are the way they are," she said. "What matters is what we're going to do about it."

Chapter Thirteen

"It's not that I think you're wrong," Jules said, fighting to keep their voice even. They didn't want to fight with Marvin, especially about something so abstract. "I just don't think there's anything any of us can do."

"You might be right," Marvin said, "but I don't think I can let things go on like this without trying. I mean, maybe nothing will change if people start speaking up, but absolutely nothing will happen if no one says anything. I feel like we have to try."

They were sitting on a bench in the atrium of the new hab dome, enough people milling around that it didn't seem conspicuous, but quiet enough to have an uninterrupted conversation. Marvin had to be at Sequins in half an hour, so Jules met up with him right after their shift. The day's sweat clung to their body uncomfortably, highlighting the difference between Marvin's powdered and perfumed state and their own dishevelled mess. How Jules looked seemed to be the furthest thing from Marvin's mind, though.

"This isn't like having a go at the open mike at Chuckles," Jules said. "I'm all for trying new things but there are real consequences here. You really think the Consortium is going to be fine with people staging protests, issuing demands? We're their employees. They can fire us, and then what happens? It's not like I planned on staying here forever, but when I leave I want it to be on my own terms. Not to mention in a way that doesn't involve a flight back that will cost me more than I've earned. And it's not like there's another game in town."

"Well, yeah, there kind of is."

"No." Jules shook their head. "For most of us, there isn't. No one is going to hire a freelance drone operator. Even the folks in the hospitality department don't have that many options. A person who can afford to start their own food cart could afford a shuttle out. For everyone else, there are only so many positions at the resort, and who knows if they would even take a Consortium reject. A lot of us are stuck here."

"It works both ways, though," Marvin said, patiently. "If they fire a load of people, who's going to do the work? The Earth-Mars run is way too long to get new staff on the fly, and there's no money if the platinum doesn't move off Mars. They need us at least as much as we need them. I think more. Lots of us think so, too. We have leverage—we should use it."

Jules shook their head again, but it wasn't really in disagreement. They knew their arguments were mainly born out of fear, but it was a legitimate concern. Sure, the Consortium would screw themselves over if they cracked down on the activist group that appeared to be forming, but it was exactly because the Consortium had been making bad decisions that people were angry. Maybe the companies behind PlatinumMars™ were willing to take a loss in the short-term to ensure long-term control over their staff. It wouldn't be the first time in the history of capitalism that had happened.

They knew Marvin, of all people, had already thought of that. He was simply willing to take the risk.

"If you don't want to be a part of this, it won't change anything between us," Marvin said, taking Jules's hand. "But I'd be lying if I said it wouldn't disappoint me. I understand that you have a lot to lose; more than I do. But everything that's important takes some risk. It was risky coming to live on Mars." His voice trailed off and he stared out across the atrium. He squeezed Jules's hand, eyes locked on an invisible point in the distance.

"I've worked a lot of shitty jobs," he said, still focussed on something only he could see. "With my skill set, that's inevitable. And I admit it, it's not bad here. Maybe that's why I care so much about this. Because it could be so much better than just 'not bad'." He turned back to Jules and looked into their eyes.

"I love Mars," Marvin said. "I love being here, and I love what I do. I love... a lot of the people here. I want this place to be as great as I know it could be. I feel like I've been given the opportunity to get in on the ground floor, at the start of something amazing. Of course it's going to be difficult now, and of course things won't work perfectly out of the gate. That's not what bothers me about the way this place is being run. Mistakes and unforeseen issues are fine. But choosing not to fix the things that are broken—that's not fine. And if no one ever speaks up, how is anything ever going to change?"

Jules didn't have an answer to that. There was quite a lot to unpack in what Marvin had said, and they weren't up to it at the end of a long day. It didn't matter anyway, because Marvin kissed them and stood.

"I have to go," he said. "Think about it, okay? Just... don't make a decision solely out of fear, that's all."

Jules watched Marvin walk to the train station, his scent somehow lingering on their creased uniform.

$\male$

Jules slept poorly that night, but it wasn't thoughts of revolution which kept them tossing and turning. They rose late on their day off, and dressed in workout clothes without spending a water ration on a shower. If they stank, so what? It would keep other people away for a while.

They took the train to the E-zone and made straight for the gym. They idly worked the resistance bands while they waited for a turn in the jumper, a high end trampoline completely enclosed by padding and elastic mats. The lower gravity meant it was a popular piece of equipment in the gym, so Jules was well limbered by the time their fifteen minutes came up.

They began with a few easy bounces, then did a couple of flips. As they worked through what had become a routine, they let their mind turn over what had been bothering them all night.

They were afraid. But they weren't afraid of getting fired and kicked off Mars. That wasn't an outcome they wanted, but they'd been in bad spots before. They were afraid of caring—caring about Mars, and more potently, caring about Marvin.

He'd very nearly said he loved Jules last night. They'd never said anything like that to each other before, even though it had become clear that they were a steady couple. Jules thought that if they hadn't been the one who was so adamant about keeping things casual, that Marvin would have finished that thought. And it terrified them.

Because they loved him, too. And they loved Mars. When they thought about having to leave, it hurt. They'd found people here who never did a double take when they said their name, people who were all reinventing themselves as much as they were reinventing the planet. It wasn't only the people, either. Jules loved the blue sunsets, the rugged landscape, even the haze of the dust storms.

They didn't want to leave Mars and they didn't want to leave Marvin.

They bounced off one wall, flipped lazily backward to spring off the opposite wall and drop to the trampoline below. Leaving Mars and leaving Marvin—those things were related, of course, but Jules had to admit that even if they'd never met Marvin they still would want to stay here.

The bell rang, sounding the end of their session in the jumper, and Jules did a couple of final bounces to bring their momentum down before climbing out of the apparatus. They towelled off on the way to the showers, their legs rubbery and their heart pounding.

By the time they got back to their tiny apartment, they'd made up their mind. It was time to start taking risks—real risks, the kind with real consequences and real rewards. They practiced a few times in the mirror before making the call.

"We need to talk."

"I want to tell you how I feel."

"Marvin, I love you."

Chapter Fourteen

Lisa Marie couldn't help but look around her, sure the entire dome could hear the thudding of her heart. No one seemed to be paying her any attention, though, and she had to remind herself that there was nothing wrong with walking through the pedestrian tunnel from Hab Dome B4 to the E-zone. She wasn't even doing anything unusual—she often went this way to The Mars Bar. But it wasn't her that was different: it was the tunnel.

The mark wasn't very large, maybe ten centimetres on the long edge at most, and it was nearly hidden by the edge of the entrance bulkhead. It was less a grand statement and more like a subtle hint to those in the know. And she was one of those people.

She'd first seen the sigil the previous week, at the crammed meeting in the bunker under Normal Bean. They'd had to start holding multiple sessions to accommodate everyone, and Smith had suggested that they abandon the location entirely. Lisa Marie wasn't sure she'd ever climb down that ladder in the storeroom again. It was almost a shame—it made such a great secret hideaway.

Over the previous weeks, Smith had slowly become the one that people looked to when a decision had to be made, and Lisa Marie had encouraged that to happen. Even though she'd started the conversation, she didn't want to be the public face of the group any more. She'd never wanted that.

Smith was a good front man and even if he was the face of the growing organization, he didn't make any decisions without her input. It was a good partnership.

At that last meeting in the underground bunker, an older woman with a Pacific Island accent had proposed the logo, a symbol that could be used to silently show allegiance to this burgeoning movement.

"I'm an electrician," she'd said as she unveiled the image. "We use this zigzag pattern to denote a resistor in a circuit diagram. I've combined it with the symbol for Mars to create this."

The resistor symbol had been used in place of the straight line in the arrow on the Mars symbol. It was simple, and easy for most people to draw. Everyone present had agreed that it would do the job.

Lisa Marie hadn't been prepared to see it in the wild, though. Until now all they had been doing was talking. Their meetings were arguably not much more than well-structured gripe sessions. But now someone had taken the time to draw the symbol in a public place—even if it was an out-of-the way spot. All of a sudden, whatever they were building was a lot more real—and a lot less in her control.

Lisa Marie kept moving, not wanting to draw attention to herself or the tiny piece of graffiti. She'd known that the number of people who were involved in this little movement she'd helped create was increasing, and had also known that there would come a time when people started speaking up on their own, engaging in activities she wouldn't know anything about. They weren't properly organized at all, even if they were organized enough that it could cause trouble.

She caught Smith's eye at a table near a group of small food stalls, and he nodded toward her slightly. She joined him, and said without preamble, "Did you know about the graffiti?"

"What graffiti?" She explained quickly, and he shook his head. "Nope, that wasn't me. Can't say I'm too sad about it, though. It's about time we stopped talking amongst ourselves and started taking action."

"Drawing on the walls isn't taking action," she hissed, eyes darting from side to side in case anyone was listening.

"Quit looking so paranoid," Smith said. "It's super suspicious." He sighed, and took a bite of his sandwich. He chewed slowly, as Lisa Marie sat still, trying not to look suspicious. Finally, he swallowed and wiped his mouth delicately with a napkin. "You're not wrong, though. If we're going to do more than just pissing off the cleaning crews we need to make sure people know what we want. Why we're upset."

"You want to send out a press release?" she asked, only half incredulous.

"No, I don't think that would help," Smith said. "It would only give the Consortium something concrete to rebut, and they've got a lot more channels than we do. Although... maybe that's not such a bad idea."

"But you just said—"

"Yeah, I know. I don't think we should make an

announcement or anything, not publicly. But maybe we should prepare a proper document, a list of the things we want to change, and ways people can get the word out."

Lisa Marie nodded, the plan starting to come together in her mind. "We aren't going to change anything overnight by demanding action," she agreed. "Especially since there's only a few of us, in the grand scheme of things." As far as she could tell, about fifty people on Mars might be aware of the discussions they'd been having. That was a tiny fraction of the total population; nowhere near enough to achieve critical mass. "No, we need to get the word out, start a real grassroots campaign."

"But organized," Smith said, leaning back in his chair.

"Exactly."

Their group was small, but diverse enough that they found someone with public relations skills, a couple of technical writers, and a performance artist who had some creative ideas for sharing information outside official channels. With two of the bartenders at The Mars Bar involved, it had become essentially a Resistance hangout.

Someone printed up simple cards with the Mars/resistor symbol, and someone else hacked a workaround to send image searches from Mars for that glyph to a public page on the nets with a write-up on the issues. If the Consortium wanted to trace the traffic they could, but it would dead-end in an anonymous uploader on Earth.

When Lisa Marie walked into The Mars Bar, Ylla was pouring drinks and gave her a nod. She found Marvin and his partner Jules talking with a group of people she didn't recognize. She hadn't really been sure about Jules; they'd never seemed to be that invested in life on Mars, but in the last few weeks things had changed. They'd thrown themselves into helping out, even if sometimes their eagerness outstripped their abilities.

That didn't matter so much—the important thing was that people were talking about what was wrong. It was the only way anything could ever change. She was walking toward the back where the pool tables were, when Jules raised their hand and beckoned her over. She joined the group, and Jules waved their handheld in her direction.

"Have you seen this?" they asked.

"Seen what?" She took the device and skimmed the text on the screen. "'Career Development Centre'? I don't know what that is."

"You did that!" Jules said excitedly. "We all did."

"It's not much, but it's a start," Marvin said, smiling at her. She still didn't know what they were talking about.

"The Consortium has opened a new department to help people move around in the various jobs here," Jules explained. "Not just moving up, but into other areas."

It started to come together. "So, just because I was hired on as a miner, I could maybe start learning robotics? Or move into administration?" Free training for a skilled career? Was that even a possibility?

"Exactly," Marvin said. "It's not that huge a change—I mean, it's still all about keeping the Consortium running, but it means they're listening. They understand that for some of us Mars isn't just the place where we work. It's where we live. And living means changing. This way we don't have to leave when we want to do something new."

Lisa Marie nodded, her mind boggling. This wasn't what she had in mind, but they were right. It was a positive change. Not just for Mars, but for her.

"Are you sure this isn't a coincidence?" she asked.

"Look." Jules passed her the handheld again.

It was a so-called news story that had obviously been lifted directly from a Consortium press release.

The Mars Consortium was initially created to exploit the natural resources of the planet, but it has recently become apparent that the group has a responsibility not only for the planet but for the people living here. The Consortium is pleased to announce the creation of a Career Development Centre, to facilitate lateral and interdepartmental career transitions for employees on Mars.

A spokesperson for the Mars Consortium told **Mars News Today**: "Mars is not simply a resource—it has become a home for the people who live there and it is imperative that the Consortium respects that. Mars is for all of us, whether we live on Earth, Luna or on Mars."

"Well, they aren't exactly shouting *Mars for Martians!* but you're right. It's a start." Lisa Marie grinned.

"You know, I like that," Marvin said. "*Mars for Martians*— it has a ring to it."

He filled everyone's glasses and they sat in contemplative silence for a while.

"Martians," Lisa Marie said. "It always sounded silly before. But now..."

"That really is what we are," Jules said. "Those of us who are staying here and making this place a real home, without always looking back to where we came from." They turned to

Marvin and Lisa Marie saw a look she didn't fully understand pass between the couple. Marvin laid his hand on Jules's shoulder and they leaned into him. "We really are Martians now," they said.

Lisa Marie lifted her beer. "I'll drink to that."